Off to Beyond

A collection of short stories

Loraine Garcia Asas

Lorela Garcia Carpio

By Loraine Garcia Asas, Lorela Garcia Carpio

ISBN
Hardbound-978-621-470-354-8
Softbound/Paperback-978-621-470-355-5
MOBI/KINDLE-978-621-470-356-2

Published by:
Poetry Planet Book Publishing House
Rosario, Pozorrubio, Pangasinan, Philippines
Contact No.: 09554960044
Email: maritesritumalta@gmail.co

DEDICATION

For Louisiane

and

Lauriane

PREFACE

This book– *Off to Beyond*, is a collection of short stories authored to primarily serve two purposes. First, to provide a compilation of sample literary works in the form of simple short stories that can be used by learners and budding writers as patterns for the Creative Writing classes. Second, to beef up the writers' creative writing prowess and consequently contribute masterpieces depicting a world where characters and situations are valid only in the readers' mind.

It shall be to the greatest pleasure of the authors should this book be used in any way that contributes inspiration and ideas to language and literature students in the aspect of their studies relative to the application of creative writing skills.

TABLE OF CONTENTS

CALLA LILY

He stopped the car from a distance, enough for him to have a good site of musing that place. It looked familiar, and he really knew it. He had been there for so many times. But looking at that familiar angle, he noticed some changes. He simply looked at his watch, and again his attention was focused on that enchanting façade. He was fascinated. It felt like an eloquent feeling was forcing him to have close contact with someone or something behind that door.

He wore his sunglasses and slowly stepped down from his car. As he opened the glass door and as he stepped inside, the same profound feeling enveloped him. But he was bothered. He was nervous as he felt the sudden beat of his heart. To hide his tremors, he simply gazed at the captivating beauty that suppressed

his strength. He touched the white roses and smelled their scent.

"Excuse me, sir. Do you want to take some of these white roses?" A soft voice interrupted him. He smiled to give back the clerk's pleasant greeting.

"No. Please give me a dozen of this kind of flower." He pointed to those flowers next to the roses.

"Sure, sir. This is our shop's prime flower!" The clerk proudly exclaimed. "Just for a while, sir." The clerk courteously added.

While waiting, he secretly grabbed that moment of having a chance to muse freely at those lovely flowers. He didn't waste a second but let time just slip away. A fragment of thoughts consolidated his memory.

He could never be wrong. He was right there in that same shop. He deeply knew it by heart and mind, but he felt he was a total stranger. There was no sign that the very same place still recognized him. Unlike the previous feeling, the feeling he had dealt with earlier was so strange. He couldn't find the right word that could describe it. He couldn't explain; he could only feel. It was just new to him. The feeling he had kept for years every time he stepped inside was pure excitement, but at that moment...he felt it was gone.

For a while, he had been disturbed by a young man who had opened the glass door. Like him, the attention of a young lady whom he believed as one of the shop's clerks was caught by him. She left what she was doing and walked closer to him. A happy smile was playing on her lips. But that smile was changed into a surprised smile while her cheeks glowed red as the young fellow handed her three stems of yellow flowers tied up with a yellow string.

"Flowers?" She exclaimed to her utter surprise.

"Yeah." The man nodded his head while grinning at her.

"You see, there are lots of flowers here!"

"I know... But look...that string of flowers I've given you is different."

The girl looked down to see the flowers only to find out he was right! A childish smile was formed on her lips. She laughed and was so pretty; how he loved to look at her that way! She could melt his heart quickly.

"What's the name of this flower?"

She disturbed his stream of fantasy.

"Your bouquet of calla lilies, sir." He was shocked. The girl brought his thoughts back to reality.

"Thank you." He said as he tried to compose himself and hide his shame. He was in the act of opening the door when he remembered –

"By the way, where's the owner of this store?" He asked.

"She's out, sir."

He nodded his head and headed his way to his car.

"Call lily..."

He murmured as he heard the answer from the young man inside the shop.

"Wow! They're pretty and nice!" The girl sweetly replied.

"From now on, this will be my favorite flower! And how I wish this will be the same kind of flower I will be holding on the day I will walk down the aisle..."

He smiled. And how he wished too that the lady to whom he would offer that bouquet of flowers would feel the same satisfaction and appreciation as the young girl had shown to that young man.

He glanced back at the store. His eyes were focused on the name of the store – Calla Lily. As the flower shop's name suggested, the shop's prime flower was the calla lily.

A blurred scene occupied his mind. He tried hard to recall what it was. It was covering his mind. In fragments, he recalled...

In that same shop he entered years ago. He was slightly upset, and that shop was his last hope. He entered quickly and called the attention of the girl whom he had mistaken for a clerk.

"Can I have a dozen of calla lilies?"

When the girl heard his voice, she stopped arranging the flowers and humbly looked at him.

"I'm sorry, sir...but we do not have that kind of flower."

He was dismayed at the girl's answer, but his face suddenly changed its expression. After a short while of staring at her face, he concluded...she was brilliantly beautiful. He smiled at her, and he saw the girl's cheeks turn red. She was surprised. He, too, was surprised. It felt so good to have this close proximity with such kind of splendid beauty...especially such kind of rare girl. He was totally stunned.

Long hair swaying freely against her shoulders, innocent brown eyes, thin lips, and rosy cheeks – the face he memorized.

He couldn't step back and leave that place, though his mind told him so. He didn't want, and he was afraid to be called a coward. He had to do that...so he took another step toward the girl he was staring at. It was

a bit of tough luck to see her. Opportunity knocked of finally meeting her and had this close encounter with the girl he longed to see.

He was mesmerized to see the angelic face he once adored. Her immaculate face and plain naivety captured him most. But when she saw him, she was too shy to meet his gaze. She held tightly the flowers she was holding. He tried to smile at her. He was lacking for words to say.

“Hello! How are you? May I know your name?”

At last, he muttered.

“By the way, do you want to have some flowers?”

He asked. Then he pulled three stems from the bouquet he was holding.

"Here... Please take these...."

He insisted. She was fairly surprised.

“Are these for me?”

She asked in disbelief. And when their eyes locked, he saw her cheeks turn red. He was amazed.

“Of course! These are for you!”

He told her in amusement.

"Well, thank you."

She said as she took the flowers from his hand.

"But I think these do not fit me...instead of her."

She said softly while handing down the flowers to the lady in front of them. He was shocked, but she gave him a sweet smile to make his worries disappear. But the lady didn't speak.

He knew that lady, but he was unsure if she could still remember him. So many years had elapsed since she last saw him. And for years, she had this special place in his heart. Yet, he could still remember the days he spent with her. Those days were the most memorable days of his life.

Still, the lady remained cold. He couldn't feel any sign that she cared about his presence. He hadn't seen any indication that she was jealous or what. He thought she had already forgotten all about him...all about them. He handed down to her the bouquet of calla lilies he was holding.

"I know this is your favorite flower; that was why I brought you this. I hope this can somehow make you feel better."

Again, she had no response...and he knew she would not. The idea that she was furious at him pounded in his mind. He felt ashamed for what he did – playing safe. Calla lilies for two girls. He just stared at her as a short interval of silence passed.

"You know that it's her favorite flower?"

The girl asked him in surprise. He answered her with a nod, still staring at the lady in front of them.

"How?"

She was curious.

“Maybe you know her, right?”

It was more of a confirmation.

“Yes.”

He uttered in a low voice. He was deeply saddened that tears welled up in his eyes.

"I always love her as a pretty young girl who really loves flowers. I used to give her three stems of calla lilies tied up with a yellow string. I love to see her smiling and blushing as she stares at and smells those flowers. Those simple expressions were enough to make me happy. But those were just simple memories…."

“You must be the man she was always talking about. You know what…she had lots of stories about you.”

A sudden realization struck him, and he found no words to say. For five long years, she was always thinking of him. She never forgot all they had before.

"She was always saying that because of me...and because of calla lilies...I always remind her of you."

In muffled words, he asked her.

"What's your name again?"

He was thankful she permitted him.

"Calla."

In total surprise and agony, he fell down to his knees. He was afraid to touch this five-year-old little girl, and he didn't even know how. And now, after five sorrowful years, he was there again to meet up with her. But it was too late...he was too late. He was back only to find out she was gone.

Sadness conquered his strength. Regrets pained him. His heart was filled with so much guilt that to cry in front of her was not. To ask for her forgiveness couldn't bring back all those he had left behind. To blame himself couldn't take away all those that pained her much. He managed to control his tears...but he could not. Pain covered his whole being.

Suddenly, he felt a small warm hand touch his shoulder.

"Don't cry. She would feel bad because she could see you crying. Don't be sad. I know she had already forgiven you because of me."

He searched for her face, and right there, he saw HER. He could never see her again. What he was holding at that moment were just memories.

But from Calla's lips, he could see her smiling. Hugging Calla's soft body made him feel he was so close to her. What he had left to her were just plain memories. But she was unfair. She left behind a living memory of her, of them the mark of her blessing.

He stood up. He was stepping slowly on his way out of the flower shop when he heard her calling him.

"Take care!"

He smiled and waved his hand goodbye.

"Please tell me more about mom tomorrow," she added.

Before he left, he stared again at that enchanting façade where years ago, he was enchanted to come inside to see the gift of fate – the one that captured his heart. He looked up and stared there for a moment. Then, he realized that he would never be tired of reading the engraved name of CALLA LILY. That name brought back so many memories.

He winked and softly wiped his eyes. He looked up at the sky, and the conclusion that she completed him made him smile.

"Calla Lily reminds you of me. But Calla reminds me of you...."

RED PAPER ROSES

I had a friend who grew up with me, somewhat like a childhood sweetheart. He was two years older than me. But we were the best of friends. We went to the same school together and went home together. When we were in elementary, he was always there for me. He protected and took care of me. When we were in high school, we studied in the school where we took our elementary. Until I was in my second year, we remained very close to each other.

He went away from me when I was in my third year. So we were not that close anymore, but I understood him. He was in college, and there would be changes that would happen.

One Saturday morning, I went to their house. I asked him, "Can you come with me? Let's eat, and let's have fun!" I told him, expecting he would come with me. Then he answered, "No, I can't. I'm going to visit a friend." I tried to understand him. But he said that not knowing those words was hurting me. Then he gave me a red paper rose. But I knew he was just calming me.

After his graduation, starting April first, he sent me a red paper rose every morning. I was happy because I thought he was still remembering me. So I kept those red paper roses in a small box.

One morning, I felt I was in love with him when I woke up. And all those red paper roses he had given me made me happy, for I thought he loved me too.

But when I knew he was courting different girls and always with them, I realized he didn't love me. But my feelings for him didn't change.

I knew why he had no time for me. He was swamped entertaining his different girlfriends.

Yes! I'm his girlfriend. His friend only, I am his friend who was silently loving him. But for him, I was just his friend.

Graduation day came, and I invited him to our graduation ball, but he didn't come. So all through the night, I waited for his coming.

When I reached our home, I ran to my room. There I found a dozen red paper roses arranged in a red vase. But, unfortunately, I was too angry with him that I ignored his gift to me.

I waited for him to call me, but he didn't. I cried until I slept. Then morning came, and he was calling me. When I heard his voice, happiness flowed upon my heart. He was requesting me to go to the seashore. I went there so fast that I thought he would ask for an apology from me or he would greet me.

I found him sitting on the sand; I sat just near him. A moment of silence passed. Then he

started to speak, "I will just tell you goodbye." Then he stood up.

I found myself running after him; I asked if he could love me if he loved me. He stopped. Anger flashed on his face, and he spoke, "Don't ask about my feelings if you do not know what you really feel." I was stunned. Those words echoed in my ear as he continued to walk.

"Wait! Can't you tell me your feelings?" He didn't answer me. Instead, he walked and left me.

Brought by hurt and pain, I threw those red paper roses he had given me.

He was out of the country for one week. But I received a piece of red paper rose every day from him. He continued sending me a bit of red paper grew. I was still angry with him, but I really missed him.

Then the day came when he went back to our country. He visited me at our house and we went to the seashore together. He handed me a piece of red paper rose. Brought by curiosity, I asked him, "Can you tell me the meaning of this red paper rose?" But he didn't reply.

Then again, for one week, I didn't see him. I thought of forgetting him.

One morning, he called me and requested me again to go to the seashore. There I went. I saw him holding a bottle of wine.

"Please, forgive me. I'm very sorry." He told me while he gave me the bottle of wine containing several red paper roses. I accepted the bottle, but I threw it into the sea.

"I don't need this!" I told him. He didn't answer me. He just looked at me with loneliness in his eyes. He swam to the sea to get that bottle. I was too late to stop him, but I did.

"Go back here! You might drown!"

But he didn't go back. He really wanted to get that bottle. Waves covered him, but he did his very best to get the bottle. He failed because he drowned, and I cried. He was dead. The men who rescued him gave me the bottle of wine, and they told me that he was still holding that bottle when they saved him.

I went home. Crying, I went to my room. I got the box where I put all the red paper roses he had given to me. I recovered those red paper roses I'd thrown in the garbage can.

I pulled one petal of the paper rose and found something was written there – *I Love You.*

I pulled again a petal of another paper rose. *I Love You.*

One...two...three... I can't count those red paper roses. And all of it stated but one, I Love You.

I cried. Loneliness filled my whole self, especially my heart. I opened the bottle of wine, and I got one paper rose. I pulled its petal, and I've read I Love You.

All those red paper roses he had given me starting April first up until the last time we saw each other contained the three precious words I longed to hear from him.

Now I understand the words that echoed in my ear, the reason why he left. And that's because he was hurting. He was afraid to tell me he loved me, for he thought; I didn't feel the same because I never minded his red paper roses. Guilt flooded my body. Regrets enveloped me.

If I only knew that he loves me too...

But I realized, on his last day, in our previous meeting, he proved and showed to me that he really loves me. Though he can't be with me, I know he's always there for me and will never leave me. He will always be at my side and will forever remain in my heart.

Life must go on, I need to live again. I need to go on. But it is tough for me to live without him at my side, knowing he can never be in my life. I can never see his smile, can never see his face, and can never tell him, prove to him, that I really do love him too. I can never see him again unless the time comes that I need to go.

But there's no reason for me not to go on. He wants me to go on. I know he's looking at me in the place where he is. If I feel pain from losing him, and he feels the same.

He died not knowing my feelings for him. I grew up with anger and jealousy, and I became too selfish. Now, I'm alone.

If I only paid attention to his red paper roses, I might know that he loves me too. If I had only listened to him on the day that he came, maybe forever he would stay at my side and forever remained in my life.

If I only...

VINDICATED

"Hello?

Who's on the line?

Hel – lo?"

One message was received.

"May I know who you are?"

Sudden pain engulfed my heart as I pressed the letters of my name.

She had many acquaintances, while I only had a few I considered friends, so I admired her not just because of her adoring face but much more of her awesome traits. Of course, she could be anybody's dream girl, but she was unaware of that.

She was a friend, and I knew I was a friend to her too. If not, why would she spare some of her precious time because of my insipidity?

She was more than just a simple friend. Nobody knew about my stupidity except her. She even knew how dumb I was.

I met her by chance, a mere coincidence that apparently I was the cause. I introduced myself and struck up my first conversation with her. I got interested in her. Thus I tried to befriend her. It was like I was a teenager, gathering information for those who knew her. But it took some time before she permitted, still I was glad. She didn't disclose anything so quickly, maybe because she didn't know me that much. The fact that we didn't see each other frequently because of work and priorities.

Though I didn't know more about her, I began to like her sincerely. Before it started as a joke, I knew I really wanted her. And I couldn't suit myself with the little things I learned about her.

Before I knew I became too hasty, I was dealing with the moment of telling her the way I could see her. She believed it was just a big joke. But she was not surprised either. I didn't know how I could convince her that she was special to me.

I tried harder to convince her – telling her I wanted to court her. Right there and then, she permitted me to know her answer. I was rejected. Though she told me she considered me a friend, I was still rejected.

Then, our friendship turned silent. It felt like she was avoiding me. Every time we saw each other, it was as if we were total strangers. But then, there were casual conversations, and it all ended there.

Maybe I was hurt when I felt rejected. On the other hand, maybe what I have done was a way of saving my personal ego.

I saw her in a crowd. I ignored her – knowing she used to ignore me too. I thought she would get jealous knowing I was right there talking with someone – not just simply talking, but it was more of a flirting. She was not affected. She didn't even bother to look.

I've tried to win her attention, wishing she could notice me. Finally, yes, she caught me, and I left her a thought and impression that later had put me in regret.

I have created a vague attachment with someone I knew as her friend through her. We spent some time talking and knowing each other. No further elaboration of what she really meant to me because I knew it was quite impossible to work out whatever intention I had for her because she was already taken. But to my utter surprise, she responded to my little tempting.

As a new friendship started to bloom, I was unaware that I was slowly losing her. I tried really hard to get rid of her from my system. I tried to ignore her and what I felt for her.

When I was rejected, I thought she was too inconsiderate. I told her everything a girl would love to hear, but she didn't give me a chance. It was all I knew 'til the moment we met again.

Her face was void of any emotion as she met my gaze. But she can still laugh and smile with our fellow friends. She was what she used to be and was not even bothered by my presence, leaving me a hint that she didn't care at all. I felt like I was a total stranger.

It pained me knowing I could never change her impression of me – that no matter how hard I tried to put things back the way they used to be, I could no longer win her trust because of my insincerity.

She knew about my last breakup. I confided to her almost everything, except for the part that it was because of her. I didn't realize her impression of me would bring me to a realization that I fell so easily – that I was never serious because of the not-so-few relationships that I've been through. I could not blame her for that thought.

I was wrong when I thought she didn't give me a chance – for she had given me enough time. If I could bring back the same things as before, I should have proven to her my real intention. Indeed, words were not enough to win her heart.

I have just shown her how insincere I was. Because I have tried to save my pride and personal ego, I dealt with a vengeance that later punished me.

She was right when she said I fell so easily – I fell for her so easily back then in our first meeting.

I wished I just suited myself with the friendship she once extended to me, than ended here craving for the same closeness I could never have again. I haven't told and proven to

her how much I love her, but everything we have had changed.

I waited for her reply, but there was none.

The girl who happened to be my friend is now gone. Though I know, she is just around...

ANGEL IN DISGUISE

As every fairy tale unfolds

There is always a sweet belief that nestles in her heart

That sometime in that pre-mortal realm

We were once angels –

Angels with only one wing

And we can only fly by embracing that one-winged angel whose half-wing matches ours.

That our stay here on earth is more of a mission

Of finding that special someone who carries the half wing that will complete ours.

He was surfing the net. And there he was again browsing his most viewed profile. As he scrolled down the button, he got curious about that single note he saw.

He had been tagged, and he was supposed to write a note with 100 truths about him. But before he erased the previous answers and entered his own, he browsed over the note, examining whether those answers were accurate. He felt something he couldn't explain.

Of the 100 truths about HER, he was caught engrossed with these...

Have you ever turned someone down? YES

She didn't mean to break his heart. It may be hurtful, but She had turned him down. So he was just allowed to be a friend.

Have you ever fallen for a friend? YES

Though it was hard, she tried hiding her feelings and pretending only to care because she was a friend.

Have you fallen out of love? YES

She believed their love was weak, which made her fall out of love. Their love had no right to fight for, or maybe there was no love at all. She ended it, for they could neither be lovers nor friends.

Has your own heart broken? YES

She had been cheated on. He said he didn't want to break her heart, but he had to say goodbye because he loved someone new. She had no choice but to let him go. And for her, it was so cruel and painful for lovers to be friends.

This was the last time she cried, thinking she had lost someone special.

Do you believe in love at first sight? YES

In her last breakup, she fought against herself to overcome the pain and managed to leave that place. She was about to leave when someone approached her and held her arm. She looked back and found an unfamiliar guy. He stared at her as he spoke, "How can I comfort you? If only I could take away the pain."

Out of curiosity, she asked him.

“Who are you?”

“It doesn’t matter now.”

Then he turned his back and walked away from her. She followed him and looked for him in the crowd but didn't find him.

From that night, she couldn’t get him out of her mind. Every day, her mind was filled with him. Yet, somehow, she had forgotten all that pained her.

Days passed by, and he was still haunting her mind. The words he said kept on repeating in her mind. It brought an intense feeling in her heart, and she was puzzled by that new feeling and the meaning of his words.

So one night, she decided to return to where they first met. Maybe, she was just out of her mind. She was there wishing he would come to see her. But he didn't come. She knew he

wasn't one of her friends or the few men she had met. For her, he was someone who changed her.

She kept returning to that place, hoping he would come and meet her. But she was always disappointed. She didn't see him. It was prayer that kept her going.

"Lord, please give me the chance to see him again. I think... I'm falling for him."

Waiting for? HIM

She was there again in that place, hoping she could see him. There she found an unfamiliar guy intently looking at her. When she met his gaze, he gallantly smiled at her as if he had known her since before.

"Forgive me..."

The little distance that parted her from him didn't matter at all. He didn't continue what he was telling her. She walked closer to him.

“Please let me know your name. I have been waiting for you, so long that I haven’t noticed the days that passed by.”

Suddenly, tears welled in her eyes.

“Don’t cry. I don’t want to see you crying. Every time, I can see you somewhere, safe to hide as I watch and love you secretly. I know you’re always here waiting. I know how sad you are, and it badly breaks my heart.”

His eyes glowed with sadness.

“I love you, and I’m not just fooling you around. It’s been so long that all I can do is just hide this feeling I have for you. But I need to say goodbye. I just can’t help myself but fall for you even more. I have no regrets if I fell for you.”

He wrapped his arms around her, and it was already goodbye.

"Please don't go...."

She ran after him and wrapped her arms around his back. And the more she held tighter, the more he became unfamiliar.

The moment she opened her eyes, he was gone. She would not wake up and loosen her grip if it were just a dream.

She was back again in that place with a secret wish to see him again. It was as if she was dealing with a dé jà Vu. She saw the unfamiliar guy, but he was not alone. She supposed that girl was his girl.

Before tears rolled down her cheeks, she decided to leave when someone approached her and held her arm. She looked back and found the man. Seeing him surprised her. He stared at her, gallantly smiling as if he had known her before, and she found that sweet.

"How did you know that I'm here?"

"It's just my instinct...a best friend's instinct."

There she laughed at his shallow humor.

There were not so few HE that she met in her life. Yet, in her searching and waiting, there were options she could take hold of.

HE who would mend a broken friendship.

HE who would mend a wounded heart.

HE who would mend a broken relationship.

HE who would mend a broken commitment and a broken heart.

HE who would mend a longing and dismayed heart.

And HE who would mend a broken HER.

So many HE that each seemed to be a good catch. So many HE that each craved for one more try.

We were once angels

Angels with only one wing

And we can only fly by embracing that one-winged angel whose half-wing matches ours.

That our stay here on earth is more of a mission

Of finding that special someone who carries the half wing that will complete ours.

She was so engrossed with her sweet belief. And to his dismay, five people already liked her status post ahead of him. So, to be different, he proudly wrote a comment.

Can I embrace you?

He browsed over her profile. She is in a relationship. He received two notifications.

She likes his comment. SHE commented on the wall post.

No...Can I embrace you?

THE HINTS OF RAIN

Tuesday morning, it was raining. I was upset and reluctant to come to school, but still, I had to. So I hurriedly stepped down from the passenger seat. Five minutes before eight, I would be late for my midterm exam. I hastily opened my umbrella, but the wind blew stronger, which made my umbrella overturn. I felt a sudden shame, and maybe out of curiosity, I looked around only to find out a girl with a pink umbrella was so amused while staring at me.

When I met her gaze, I saw her eyes smiling before she retracted her sight away from me. A childish smile was innocently playing on the twisted corner of her lips. I sighed and smiled. "What a day!" I said to myself as I shook my head in amusement. I didn't pay much attention to the other students who had witnessed that funny scene. Who wouldn't laugh or even smile when they see an umbrella that seems to be catching the rain droplets? But my mind was captured by that girl.

Whenever it was raining, I didn't know why I always thought about that girl. And what surprised me most was a strange feeling that I was hoping to see her again somehow—wishing that that rain was a clue that she was just very near me.

Every time the rain fell, I felt like heaven was against me. But while walking inside the campus, I was silently looking for someone. With my eyes wide open, I secretly looked at those girls holding pink umbrellas, wishing she was one of them. But to my disappointment, I always failed. I didn't know how this feeling got the power to have control over me. I hadn't found a chance to see her again, but her face always haunts me.

Then one day, the sky turned black. The wind blew stronger, hinting that rain would fall in a bit of time. I slowly walked along the corridors when I raised my gaze, and instantly, I saw her face. I saw her again! Like the first day, her face was still lovely. Her innocent eyes seemed to be always smiling, the same as her pink lips.

I knew a smile was forming on my lips as I carefully snatched a look at her. She was walking along my way, and I had almost touched her hair when she passed by. She was too close that made my world spin slowly. But it seemed she didn't notice me. I looked back to give her a short glance and saw her enter the same room I had attended for my previous class. The feeling of seeing her again was divine. I was so happy to participate in my next class, knowing she was right there in my favorite room.

At night, lying alone in my bed, I always returned to the day I first laid my eyes on her. I believed – before, and after seeing her, there was always a hint of rain. Yet, somehow, I could secretly muse at her when I saw her silently sitting inside my favorite room. I was always there, silently peeping through the windows while passing on that room.

I want to scold myself for having such kind of strange reaction. It was an ordinary Tuesday morning. I didn't think I would find a chance to see her again. I felt a sudden heat flood my body when I saw that familiar pink umbrella. Little by little, I found a beautiful site on seeing her face. It wasn't just an ordinary chance to see her but a sweet surprise of finally meeting her. She stopped in front of me. I also stopped, not knowing why she did that.

Then I heard somebody call my name. That was the only time I had paid attention to the guy beside her who was holding her pink umbrella. He was smiling at me. Though I was shocked, I managed to smile back at him. We exchanged short words of friendly greetings.

When my old friend talked about her, I looked at her. I saw how she blushed, and I felt something strike my heart. For the first time, I got to look closer at her face. Then the realization that she looked familiar tightly squeezed my mind.

By just simply looking at her, I realized I knew her. All the way, I didn't notice that I had known her for so long. I blamed myself for those times I became careless when I saw her. I have known her since before. That I had met her so many times before that rainy day, she mused me and gave me a hint that she, too, had known me.

Seeing her with another guy holding her pink umbrella to protect her against the rain secretly pained my heart. The feeling was just new to me. And I had no idea of having such kind of feeling.

After that bittersweet surprise of finally meeting her, I couldn't understand why I felt an unexplainable disappointment, a sudden feeling of being a loser. Who was her to have the power over me? Did she mean something to me? Maybe I couldn't just accept that painful honesty of seeing her with another guy. Perhaps I couldn't accept that she ignored me when I was introduced to her. I was very eager and excited to know her, but she just gave me a simple smile.

I was getting unreasonable. By the way, in the first place, I forgot to ask myself, who was I to feel that way? Who was I to expect something from her?

But when the time came that I had established a clearer image of her, chances seemed to be against me. For almost a couple of weeks, I didn't see her. Yes, it was raining, and as usual, I again wished to see her. I was silently praying that the hints of rain wouldn't fail me. But the clues were getting darker. The rain didn't mean anything during those days. The rain once failed me, and I felt hopeless.

The days I had spent my time in our home made me desperate. We had no classes – a hindrance that meant I couldn't see her.

When classes resumed, I felt my excitement and hopes of seeing her once more turn weaker. There was a sudden change that made me confuse. But the realization that I badly missed made my world spin slowly. Why was I feeling that way?

I was again on my way to my next class when I saw a familiar image. My defenses were all torn apart. She was right there in front of me, shyly smiling at me. So, of course, I smiled back at her. And it was so strange for a guy like me to feel that my cheeks turned red. I didn't know if she had noticed that. I prayed she did not.

I secretly looked at her as she passed in front of me. Then, I realized she didn't change. The rain didn't give any sign, but I met her again.

One day, I saw that familiar pink umbrella again. She was walking alone. I was running after her. And when she heard I was calling her name, she stopped. Maybe unconsciously, she waited for me as I approached her. I offered to hold her umbrella. Though she didn't utter her permission, I slowly got it from her. We walked together. We were walking silently. It seemed no one wanted to speak. Finally, when she was near their room, she walked ahead of me. All I did was stare at her. I let my words leave unsaid like my heart left broken.

Then I remembered the day she didn't look at me anymore. The day she didn't stare at the window. Maybe I was just desperately assuming that she used to stare at me secretly before. What if she was looking for someone then and there? Yes, I was always there. I was also looking for someone, and I didn't mind her. I knew I had seen her staring every time our eyes met. But I thought it was just a coincidence; besides, back then, I didn't care.

I guessed that was a couple of years ago. Though I already knew the name that struck my heart and though I had realized what she meant to me, I didn't know if I had to confide that to her.

The world was so against me. Heaven was so against me. Though I did not wish to see her, I could always see her pink umbrella. But she was not alone. There was always someone who was protecting her against the rain.

Meeting her once in a while, the pain of finally realizing that she had won over her frustrations in keeping whatever she had for me made me feel the greatest pain because I loved her—and knowing that just put me in regrets. I didn't know when and how to stop. I loved her with no assurance that she would love me in return.

I tried to ignore her. I tried not to mind our meeting, as if I didn't meet her. The heaven and the rain always gave me hints that I would be hurt when I saw her. But what pained me most was the rain would imply that I would be hurt when I saw her with someone...someone who used to hold her pink umbrella.

No one knew that I was aching in pain every time the rain fell. The hints of rain always reminded me that I once failed.

Tuesday morning, and it was raining. I was upset and reluctant. I hurriedly stepped down from the passenger seat. Five minutes before eight, I would be late. I hastily opened my umbrella, but the wind blew stronger, which made my umbrella overturn. I felt a sudden shame, and maybe out of curiosity, I looked around only to find out a girl with a pink umbrella was so amused while staring at me....

DE NOVO...

(Once More)

It's better to tell someone "I love you" though you're not sure that your love would be reciprocated than lose someone you love and regret someday because of letting that one valid love slip away.

It was the night before our graduation. I was talking with him in our garden.

"I don't want to go... But my father decided to send me to America... for my college years."

I tried not to cry, but I was very sad then. A moment of silence passed, then I spoke again.

"What will I do? I don't want to be away from you." More tears flowed from my eyes. I saw his eyes sparkle, but I knew those were the tears he didn't want to shed. Then, he laughed.

"It's okay. It's not yet goodbye. We're going to see other again. Promise... I'll wait for you," he said, smiling.

“Promise.” He said as he raised his right hand to swear. “But promise me also that you'll wait for me.”

He was my best friend. From our childhood days, we were always together. We were studying at the same school, and we were classmates. He was just ten months older than me. He was also like a brother to me. I am the only child and felt all the love I've longed for from a brother or a sister – from him. He was always there to help and support me. He always made me laugh and smile. That's why being away from me enveloped my whole being, especially my heart, with sadness.

Our graduation day came. I was so excited to see him and hear the words he would tell me. Because when he reached their home, he phoned me to say that he had something to say to me after our graduation rites. A surprise, he exaggerated to me. But when I saw him, something ached in my heart. I saw him embracing another girl. I ran away from that place, and I walked straight to my bedroom when I reached our home. Then, I realized I loved him. I cried because, for all I knew, he was courting that girl. He was not a playboy but what pained me more was the thought that he had been hiding from me that he had a girlfriend.

I admit that I used to tease him, but during those times, I couldn't explain why something was aching in me every time I did that. Now, I knew... I loved him.

Night came, and I needed to go outside my room to entertain our guests. It was a party for my graduation and, at the same time – a *Despedida.* I was thinking of him and wishing, and he felt the same way.

Then, to my surprise, he was there in our house.

"Hello!" he greeted me. "Why did you not wait for me after our graduation?" he asked. I've found no words to say. He smiled. "But anyway, I have a big surprise for you!"

"You know what? I'm going to study in America. I'll go with you!" he said, embracing me. All my sadness disappeared. "Really?" I hugged him too.

That was the most memorable and happiest part of my life. Though he didn't say he loved me, I believed he could also love me in return.

I was so excited to go to the airport. Last call. But why was it that he was not still there? I felt nervous and wanted to cry. Then, as I walked toward the departure area, I heard someone calling me. I looked back... and saw him. I smiled and ran back to meet him.

"Sorry. But I cannot go with you. My mother doesn't want me to go. Please, understand me.", he begged me. I didn't speak, but I cried.

“Please don’t cry. Promise... I’ll wait for you...”, he said. But my father headed me toward the departure area.

“I’m sorry..." he shouted. But when I looked back, I saw the girl he embraced in our school walking toward him. Then, the door was closed. I went to America with my heart broken and myself incomplete...

A month later... I received a letter from him. “I am really sorry. To be away from you, I can’t take it. But I need to understand and accept the circumstance. I know you understand me. Take care of yourself and promise me...you’ll be back...for me. Because... I love you.”

After I read his letter, I cried. Honestly, I didn’t believe him because I thought; he didn’t love me, but the girl I saw at the airport. And maybe, she was one of the reasons he didn't want to go.

Six years had passed, but I didn't answer any of his letters. During those years, we had no communication. I missed him because I still loved him. But every time I thought of that girl, my heart hardened. I had no information about him too. Another year had passed when I decided to go back home.

When I returned to our country, all seemed to be different. I've missed all the things I used to have and do here. But before I went home, I went first to their house. Nothing had changed, but it seemed it was full of sadness and regrets.

I pushed the doorbell, and an old woman came out. I could still remember her. She was their caretaker.

"Ma'am, may I help you?" she asked me politely.

"Don't you remember me?" I asked her. She thought for a moment.

"Yes! I remember you." She invited me to get inside the house. Then, she handed me something.

I went home. I unwrapped the box the older woman had given me. Full of curiosity, I found a CD and played it in the player. But why did I feel something ached in my heart? I sat down and listened to the song. I smiled. It was my, instead... our favorite song. The music stopped. After a few seconds, I heard a voice...his voice.

"Why didn't you come back for me? Didn't you believe that I love you? I'm sorry I didn't have enough courage to tell you this. How are you? Me? I miss you. I have now fulfilled my

dream to be a vocalist. I now have my band. I made this song for you...."

Even though you're not here

I still love you

I wish I could hold you again

For me to fulfill

All the wasted time s and chances

Please come back to me...

And the music stopped.

I found myself crying as I recalled the words of the old lady.

"Their family migrated to America. He has a wife now. He wanted to give this song to you when he became a vocalist in their band. He waited for you; every day, he sang your favorite song...."

THE PAST

It's a lie to say you've let go of the past, and nobody can just let go of memories. Each tear is an unforgettable memory, each smile is an undeniable mark, and each heartbreak leaves an unerasable scar because there is no such thing as forgetting... just accepting.

There she was, standing at the school gate waiting for a tricycle ride when I first saw her. She possesses such exquisite beauty – big brown eyes, cute nose, fair complexion, bouncing long night-black hair, and glimmering lips that seem to communicate an exotic smile that only she could create.

She was in her casual get-up – skinny black jeans, violet lady's-cut T-shirt, and purple bronze sandals. I walked toward her in apparent apprehension. She smiled. Oh my God! That wonderful smile. I couldn't forget that smile. I stood beside her, uneasy about starting a conversation. Time was so swift that it was too late when I noticed her waving to the approaching tricycle, and she immediately took a ride.

For almost three months, I was like a secret agent working on espionage over her.

I need to know her name. I have to ask her if we have already met somewhere or if she remembers me at least as an acquaintance. I have so many things to inquire about from her.

I was pretty sure she was the one I loved back then.

And I am dying to discover if she remembers me as the one who used to own her heart.

I have to get straight from her if she remembers the past... our past.

Sunday morning. I went to the nearby grocery store to buy some important house stuff.

It was as if a certain force directed my sight to where she stood. Then, at last, I saw her again. And so I decided that I wouldn't let that opportunity slip away. As I approached her, something seemed to have glued me to where I was standing. I saw a handsome, decent-looking, affluent man heading toward where she was.

The man gave her a quick smack on her right cheek. She smiled. My God! That smile! That exotic smile, I believe only she could create, almost killed me! The next thing I knew was that she and that man walked away very sweetly in the usual lovers' holding hands.

For almost three weeks after that incident, I did not see her. Though I had never made myself absent from my job of spying on her, I still failed to satisfy my heart with at least a minute of sighting her. I was like losing my sanity. My desire, or should I call it an obsession, to see her again had nearly reached its peak, and I felt I was set into a do-or-die situation.

One afternoon, as I was setting myself in my usual "espionage" near the school gate, I overheard a group of high school boys conversing with each other about a topic that caught my attention.

"I'm tending to lose interest in our English class."

"Me too. I don't like the substitute teacher. How I wish Ma'am Reyes would get well the soonest so that she could come back to teach us."

"I wish that too, but Ma'am Carlos said Ma'am Reyes might stay for about another week in the hospital."

"Is that so? For sure she'll be required to have bed rest after her month-long hospitalization."

“Uhmmm, excuse me guys, I overheard you’re talking of a sick teacher...."

I started with apprehension. *I mean your English teacher is sick. Did I hear it right?*

“Yes sir. Ma’am Reyes had been on leave for nearly three weeks now.”

"Ma'am Reyes..." I was blank, wondering. My heart was growing fast into suspicion that it could be her. "You mean Ma'am Reyes... the lady with an exquisite beauty – big brown eyes, cute nose, fair complexion, night-black bouncing long hair, and...."

“kissable lips that create the best smile ever!” one of the boys uttered.

“Ummm, is she your teacher?” I opted to get some information from the students.

“Yes sir, our English teacher.”

“Best English teacher rather...for us.”

"Ummm, sir, are you her secret admirer?" one of the boys queried.

The other boys started teasing me. "Are you related in any way to Ma'am Reyes?"

I felt cornered. I was puzzled. "Ummm, no... I mean yes...yes, in the past... yes."

So, you're Ma'am Reyes' ex! As in ex-bf! Too bad, sir! You let the jackpot slip away! And the three boys burst into deafening laughter.

"No! No! She's not my...." I was still trying to explain, to correct their interpretation, but they went on laughing as they headed to the computer shop across the street.

I got sleepless nights. It's almost a month since I was not seeing her. I went back several times to get more information from the three naughty boys in school, but it seemed I was always on the wrong timing.

First Thursday of February. I was driving to the next village to meet my old-time friends for a drinking spree when suddenly, as if by a jest of fate. I saw her! Yes, it was her!

I hurriedly went off my car to approach her. I have to do this now. I must assemble a tremendous amount of courage to force myself near her. This is a do-or-die situation! It's now or never.

I won't let the jackpot slip away!

"Ummm, Good day Ms. Reyes!" I approached her with such obvious tension. She smiled. I tried to keep myself relaxed.

"I'm happy to see that you're okay now."

I noticed her raise an eyebrow.

"Ummm, I learned that you got hospitalized...Ummm,...from the students... Ummm..." Too bad, my tongue seemed not to be so cooperative that moment that I had a hard time putting all the things I wanted to say into words.

"Do you have a son or daughter in our school?" she asked.

"Ummm...none. None yet. Ummm, I'm single." I knew my answer sounded awkward.

"Oh, I'm sorry. Anyway, thank you for your concern, sir. I have to get inside now. It's time for my medicines."

"Ummm, ma'am, is this your residence?" I bravely asked. Again, I knew it was awkward to have asked what was obvious.

"Yeah. Bye."

"Bye for now...." I was so sorry for myself. She did not even mind knowing my name.

From then on, I kept driving around their village every morning, hoping that I could take her for a ride to school. But unfortunately, for several days, I wasn't successful.

Friday afternoon, I got the 'one in a million chance of seeing her as she was hurrying home. I smiled at her, and she smiled back! My God! If that precious smile of hers could kill, I'll surely be dead on the spot! I hurriedly approached her and offered help in carrying her bags, which I learned from her were containing formal themes that she would bring home for checking.

"Thanks a lot, mister. Just hand my bags to that man approaching us."

"Hi, sweetie!" the man kissed her on the cheek and turned to me to get the bags of formal themes. I blankly handed the bags to the guy, uneasy about the situation. Then, finally, I smiled painfully at them and opted to return to my car.

"Hey, mister!" I heard her calling, so I walked back toward them. "Thanks again for your help. By the way, this is Roland."

The guy offered me a handshake, and I could hardly recall the following incident; I didn't even know how I got to drive my wheels home.

That night was the longest night for me. I couldn't wait to see the day break to end my insanity. I was firm with my plan to talk with her to put things back in their proper places.

"Good morning, mister! 'Seemed something serious brought you here," she uttered as a greeting in her usual killer smile as she was opening the gate.

"Yes, Ms. Reyes... Not only serious... but deadly serious."

She led me to the garden set. There was such a deafening silence between us. I was trying to observe her, and I guess she was in no way uneasy about the situation. She was the first who break the silence.

“Can I offer you any sort of drinks... uhmmm coffee, iced tea, or fruit juice?”

“No thanks. Don’t bother.”

“So what brought you here?”

For a while, I was rattled. I didn't know how to start my litany. But I knew I had to take this opportune time to inquire about everything from her. This is a now-or-never chance. So I gathered much courage and started...

“I have long been wishing for this time to talk with you. Uhmmm... ahh... I... I can't explain why...but it's how I...how I felt when I first saw you...."

She was looking straight at me.

“It seemed that I have known you before... uhmmm...uhmmm...maybe...uhmm... in the past. I believe we have known each other in the past...."

"Are you sure? If it was true, then it's such a cute situation."

"I know this is hard to believe. But, don't you feel a surge of familiarity between us? I mean, Ms. Reyes... I'm appearing crazy before you... hmmm...but it's okay, I'll still go on... don't you remember me? Uhmmm...Couldn't your heart recognize me?"

I'm so sorry, mister. You don't look drunk... but how you talk seems to project your drunkenness."

"Oh, I'm very sorry to have upset you. Can I go back some other time for a visit?"

"It's pretty unbecoming, mister so I have to say no. I'm engaged."

I pulled an extra ounce of courage and said, "Engaged but not yet married."

"But I'll surely be married. You're a joker!"

"No. I'm not. And never I was. Would you take it as a joke if I ask you now to marry me?"

She paused for a while. I saw her eyebrows wrinkled. Then, looking straight into my eyes, her look piercing through every nerve she spoke.

"You're too confident, mister... as before. Maybe this time I will have to take it as a joke. Innumerable years back, you asked me to marry you... and I said 'yes'... that was because I didn't know you were just joking then. Everything about the wedding preparation seemed fine, and I guess I was the happiest woman on earth. But my happiness turned out to be the most excruciating pain a woman in love could ever feel."

I was shocked. Those statements of hers were so spontaneous, strange, but penetrating. I said nothing. I was blank. I didn't understand it, but I got it. I felt as if a colossal ball of force had rocketed into my being to pilot myself into the past.

"You were asking me if I didn't feel any surge of familiarity between us. You were asking me if my heart couldn't recognize you as the one I loved back then. Would you take it as a joke if I say yes...?"

I was in utter detainment of what she was trying to lead to. So I cannot give voice to what I would like to say...to explain...

I was frozen back in time. Numbness lodged into my whole being.

"Yes... my heart recognized you from our first encounter... at the school gate, that fateful day when I was in my casual get-up – skinny black jeans, violet lady's-cut T-shirt, and purple bronze flat shoes; and you walked toward me in obvious apprehension. Yes... my heart recognized you as the one I loved back then, the one I was supposed to marry...."

Her bitter tears begin to show. I can't withstand the situation of seeing her in agony.

"Now, Louie, I'll be the one to ask you. Didn't your soul recognize me as your would-be-bride? Didn't you recognize me as the woman you didn't give a damn about on our wedding day?"

WHEN LOVE HAS FADED

How will you know that your love has faded? It's when you see each other, and everything is quite normal, nothing special... no racing of heartbeat... no flushing of cheeks...no twinkling of eyes... no tensed movements... no more 'what ifs' and 'how I wish'...just contentment – that you're through with that person.

Bus Terminal.

Hundreds of passengers moving to different provinces in the North tended to become impatient for their departure. Some children were playing; others were crying. Vendors were busy with their respective businesses – peanuts, corn, apples and oranges, quail eggs, donuts, candies, sunglasses, homemade stuffed toys, et cetera.

"Hi!"

I was surprised when a particular stranger approached me. However, I recognized him at once.

“Oh, hi!”

“Uhmmm...are you going to Baguio?”

“Yes, for at least a week-long vacation.”

“Uhmmm...with your husband, of course. Uhmmm... where is he?” he inquired while looking around.

“Yes, of course, he wanted anyway to check if our rest house there needs some sort of repair. He already brought to the bus our baggage.”

"Calling all passengers of Bus 72 bound to Baguio...."

“We got to go ahead...

“Uhmmm...take care.”

“Bye.”

I was in my second year of college when I first met him. He was in his third-year level taking Business Administration while I was into AB Psychology. He used to be a 'campus figure' – tall, mestizo, with a guy-next-door image, reasonably intelligent, and darling of the crowd!

"Vivian, may I bring you home?"

My God! This couldn't be true! He approached me! My heartbeat started racing, and I felt how hot my cheeks were turning! I tried hard to compose myself.

"Ah, I'm waiting for my cousin Betty; her Pol Sci class will be dismissed at 5:30!"

"Oh, it's okay! So we'll wait for Betty."

It was the very first close encounter we had. Then, out of the blue, he approached me! Oh my God! It was a dream come true! Almost every *collegeala* on the campus dreams of being close to him!

“Ah, uhm... we’re still going to the bookstore to buy a pocketbook," I said, trying to drive him away with such an alibi.

"Nice, I'm also going to buy a pocketbook there. So, I'll join you and Betty," he exclaimed confidently and teasingly as if he was boasting that I couldn't get off him with my alibi.

So that was really the start. The following Sunday, he visited me at home. He brought me a dozen flowers, a number of chocolates, and a blue magic cuddly bear!

“You’re not the type whom I can just court around. May I come in?” He said as he winked his eye.

There went the racing of my heartbeat again. I was aware that my movements seemed so awkward, but I couldn't help hiding my apparently tense movements.

“Relax...” He teased me and he smiled so sweetly.

That was one of the most nostalgic days of my life!

After almost a year of courtship, I answered him. I was thrilled, maybe happier than anyone else. Then, he came every Sunday afternoon with Goldilocks, Dunkin Donuts, chocolates, pastries, or other sweet stuff. Since then, I marked every Sunday as a Special Day, just as my heart waited for his coming. To top it off, I fell in love – maybe for the very first time with him, whom I thought would love me as I loved him. For once in my life, I felt whole!

I felt whole because I started to attach my worth to him. My sense of happiness and completeness correlated to his every visit, phone call, or text message. But then, I suddenly did not know who I was anymore.

All along, happiness and void seemed to besiege my being. I can't explain why. I actually have no idea. It was utterly unexplainable feelings that haunted me day and night. Our one year of love, if it was really love for him, was like a labyrinth that seemed to me a unicursal affair, a complicated torturous situation glazed by his secrets, an intricate state of love that I had never imagined...yet I chose to stay amidst confusion and incomprehension.

Then he graduated. He was hired as a junior executive in a particular company where his uncle was one on the Board of Directors.

The weekend-scheduled visit started to dissipate. Even the calls and messages turned conventional and dull—excuses accumulated to hundreds or maybe thousands of forged words adorning storied situations.

Does this happen to everyone who falls into the captivity of love? So many times, I tried to resolve the grueling labyrinth I was stuck into. I kept on unlocking the passcode of my mental capacity to decode the truth if I was in love with the person or just in love with love.

In the vast space of skepticism and affliction, he didn't show up anymore. So our relationship – if it was something that mattered to him had no closure.

I was awakened from my reminiscing by gentle kisses on my forehead, "Sweetie, wake up now. We're already here."

"Yeah. We'll surely have a good vacation here. I love you...." I said while trying hard to open my half-closed eyes.

"We've just gotten to the terminal, we haven't reached our rest house yet and you're starting to get too romantic, sweetie..." my husband went on jokingly.

"There you go again with your teasing! I said smilingly.

But how do we really know that our love has faded?

Is it when you see each other and everything is quite normal? Is it when you confirm that nothing seems extraordinary? No more racing of heartbeat? No more flushing of cheeks? No more twinkling of eyes? No more trace of tensed movements? No more 'what ifs' and 'how I wish'? and all that embraces your whole being is nothing but just advertence and contentment– that your life's chapter is through with that character?

I believe YES. That was really how. And I'm quite contented that I was through with Orlan.

FINDING THE MISSING PIECE

There was this myth that we knew how to love even before we were born... that in the pre-mortal realm where we came from before being held here on earth, we already found the love of our life, well – the love of our eternity. And that half of our heart was given to that person for safe-keeping...and in turn, they gave half of theirs to us... that a big part of our being here on earth is finding that special someone who carries half of our heart to complete us...

She reread that part of that fiction...and again...and again. Then, at the back of her mind, something seemed to shout approval to such a mystical thought. So she purposely read that myth again, this time with such an unexplainable convinced spirit, and memories of the past flooded her being.

It was a semestral break then. Her aunt took her on vacation in the province. There, she seemed to enjoy life so much; after the toilsome first semester, she could find a way out of the headache-inviting computations and transactions for her Accounting subject. However, since she entered her sophomore year, she had this questionable feeling of wanting to hate Accounting. She had just gone to the seashore with her cousins, who were only in their elementary grades, when someone came hurrying, trying hard to approach her. “Miss, pwede ba makapamangkot?” The guy in trunks and white sando offers a handshake. Confusion registered on her face, so one of her cousins translated, "Ate, pwede raw ba Siya magtanong?” She automatically gave a blank smile to the guy.

From then on, the guy started dropping by her grandfather’s house to visit her. They used to talk about a lot of things– sensible things. Since she was in her second year in BS Accountancy and he was in his third year in Marine Transportation, they’ve got pretty good exchanges of information about their respective courses. He used to talk about maritime stuff while she talked about economics and the matter of debit and credit. One time, he explained the topic concerning buoyancy and she was so amazed! So, at the back of her mind rang that he was the type of guy she liked – a gentleman who always talked with sense, was good-looking, wealthy, and intelligent!

The last Sunday of May came, and the sem break was over, which meant parting ways for the two of them. They boarded the same ship going back to Manila for the start of the second semester. When they reached the port after fourteen hours of travel, they parted ways with a silent promise of keeping in touch... always. A pat on her shoulder waved the first pinch in her heart as he smilingly walked off.

For quite some time, they enjoyed a sort of unconfirmed long-distance "friendship" until things gradually collapsed, and she thought he was not the one carrying her missing piece.

*****

Her second love encounter was nostalgic. It was the time when she was still nursing a dismayed heart when a letter was handed to her. She was puzzled upon handling the letter, and when she opened it, she turned more baffled as she read what was scribbled there.

The first time I saw you, you were standing in the rain. Then, something about you made me look again... the way you let the rain fall down on you... the way that you smiled when your eyes met mine.

“Quite familiar!" she thought. And even though she would like to laugh at it (for those were but lines from a popular song), she just couldn't. Instead, she continued perusing the lines...

I'll always remember, and I'll never forget how you took my breath away the first time we met. No matter what happens, no matter what you do... I'll always remember the first time I saw you.

Taken aback, she felt as if something sharp seemed to have spotted the core of her heart. Ridiculous, it may seem, but she was moved by each line. And a sudden surge of happiness sprang in her sorrowful heart. She couldn't explain what it was that she felt at that very moment. She excitedly brought her sight to the lower portion of the stationery paper to discover who had sent her the letter rather than the song...

"Who's this?" and in utter confusion and wonder, she put back the stationery paper in its

1-4-3 fold.

Early that evening, she was disturbed by a gentle knocking at the door. Surprise enveloped her being upon seeing that handsome, tall guy with a fair complexion handing her a box of three red roses, trying to win her heart in that first meeting with his smile which she thought was the sweetest she had seen – ever!

From then on, her sad love story changed. This handsome, fair, tall guy was always on guard for her every move like a spy. She admired his powerful weapon– the facility to write sweet love letters. The guy was so in love… so much in love… deeply in love with her. He used to bargain about giving up his religion for marriage with her. Yes, he even admitted he would die for her!

And then again, her heart was moved, for no one yet had been in love as such to her. She was happy, maybe happier than before. But eventually, she felt like something was still wrong with her…that something was missing that was holding her back from being the "truly complete" person she could be. And so she refused the love he offered, believing that he was not the one carrying her missing piece.

*****

In her fantasies, she imagined finding who it was that she was missing. She'd close her eyes and live in a make-believe world with her one true love. She held on to her fantasies and tried hard to make them a reality by filling the void she was feeling in her heart with things she thought could bring her there.

One cold twilight in February, she thought she'd finally found him, he who was carrying half of her heart which God gave away. The funny thing was, she found him just as she had stopped looking for him. Fate had introduced to her another one– a gentleman from the business world, intelligent and well-off. She tried to convince herself that she was finally whole!

Yet, in the end, two years seemed to suffice to decide that the piece she thought had been perfect finally was actually not... for love was not truly there. For some unidentifiable reasons, she couldn't accept him. It was difficult for her to let go of him, for he seemed so right... but eventually, she had to.

And he wrote with a distressed heart:

"You might not need me now... not tomorrow, maybe not ever. But if even for an instance you realized you need me, remember that during that moment, I'm just here."

Then again, she was puzzled. What if he really was her missing piece? It was possible! Why not? He could be that man she was missing! He who is well-off, a business-oriented man who drives his wheels from an exclusive subdivision to his office in Manila. He who was a man of intelligence so engrossed in talking about politics, election concerns, party-list systems, documented protests and strikes, and even health-related issues. No time seemed dull with him, for he was really bright and logical and true to himself. It wasn't difficult to love him anyway. He was so sweet and thoughtful, and he was the only one who called her "my angel, my love."

She became curious about something profound within the myth she had read. It was really possible – for in the said pre-mortal realm, each man and woman was an angel. Accordingly, each angel was being sent here on earth for a human journey carrying the other half of someone else's heart. No matter what, every angel will always consciously or unconsciously search for the owner of the other half of the spirit they carry. In greatest probability, she could be his angel, as he used to believe. But the thought that he could be her angel, she denied! And he was hurt... deeply hurt.

Their very last meeting was a treat for her at one of the famous cake shops in town. So they ended up as friends. That's how they intended to start, anyway. He handed her a little note which she immediately kept in her jeans pocket.

“Aren’t you going to read it now?”

"I'll just read it at home tonight... for a 'surprise effect.'

That night, tears welled in her eyes as she read his note:

"You are to me an angel; that's true

Someone I loved, but didn’t love me too.

Yet, if there is one thing I wouldn’t regret

It had to find my angel, and that is you...."

Her mind turned blank. She didn't know what to think or what to feel. Could it be possible that they already loved each other in the pre-mortal realm? Was she the angel he knew and loved back then? She felt so sorry that she couldn't recognize him as the one carrying her missing piece.

Twenty-five years swiftly passed.

"Mr. Capistrano..." the surgeon started to speak.

"Yes, doc. How's my wife?"

"The greatest power from above has worked on her. The operation was successful."

"Praise the Lord!"

"By the way mister, the heart donor had it as his last wish to have this note be handed to the patient with whom his heart was given."

My angel, my love,

I hope by the time you read this note, you are in your best shape. Twenty-five long years did not erase my greatest wish that you would one day recognize me. I prayed that God grant my heart to fit perfectly with yours... so that our journey here on earth would not be in vain.

As her sight moved to that line that bears the letters of her donor's name, tears of discernment welled from her eyes. She had proven the myth. At long last, though it was by his death, she found the one that carried half of her heart which God gave away. Nonetheless, she didn't want to deny she was finally complete... just the way she was...back then, during that one cold twilight in February when she first found her missing piece.

ABOUT THE AUTHORS

LORAINE G. ASAS had been a college instructor handling Communication Arts and Literature subjects at the Immaculate Conception International College of Arts and Technology.

She obtained her degree, Bachelor Of Arts In Mass Communication, Major In Broadcasting (AB-Broadcasting) at Bulacan State University.

She has earned her complete academic requirements for the degree Master in Public Administration major in Fiscal Administration (MPA-Fiscal Administration) from La Consolacion University Philippines.

She is currently connected with the Regional Trial Court of Caloocan City as Court Interpreter III.

LORELAI G. CARPIO is an English teacher for 25 years.

Shc has carned her complete academic requirements for the degree Doctor of Philosophy in English Language and Literature (Ph.D.-ELL) from La of Arts in Education, major in English (MAE-English) as *magna cum laude.*

She is currently in the service of the Department of Education- Sta. Lucia National High School as a Master Teacher I (MT I) handling research subjects.

www.ingramcontent.com/pod-product-compliance
Lightning Source LLC
LaVergne TN
LVHW010114170826
845678LV00012B/2394